THE ADVENTURES OF SHERLOCK BONES

CASE FILE #1: DOGGONE

Lauren Baratz-Logsted

Month9Books

THE ADVENTURES OF SHERLOCK BONES, CASE FILE #1: DOGGONE
by Lauren Baratz-Logsted
All rights reserved. Published in the United States of America by Month9Books, LLC.
No part of this book may be used or reproduced in any manner whatsoever without written permission of the publisher, except in the case of brief quotations embodied in critical articles and reviews.

Cloth ISBN: 978-1-945107-30-6 ePUB ISBN: 978-1-945107-31-3
Mobi: 978-1-945107-32-0

Published by Tantrum Books for Month9Books, Raleigh, NC 27609
Cover illustration by Meaghan McIsaac
Cover design by Najla Qamber Designs

For Georgia McBride:
longtime publishing friend, all-time publishing
visionary

THE ADVENTURES OF SHERLOCK BONES

CASE FILE #1: DOGGONE

CHAPTER ONE

There I was, lounging on the little patch of grass outside my home. It's a good spot from which to watch the world go by. And on a sunny day, it's a good spot for a nap. Being a cat, I don't tan the way humans do. But when the sun hits my fur, it's such a cozy, safe feeling.

I had recently returned, just a few months ago, from the Cat Wars. Like most wars—whether between humans or animals; within a species or between species—the Cat Wars were set off by a disagreement between two sides. One side says or does something the other doesn't like, and before you know it, rather than talk it out, everyone is fighting.

Of course, I had not fought in the Cat Wars; I'm not much of a fighter. I'm a doctor, a surgeon to be exact, one who operates on the wounded. But in wars, even non-fighting doctors can suffer injuries. And so it was that when my leg had been hurt, and it became clear that I would have a permanent limp for the rest of my lives, I was sent home to London, where I live alone except for the presence of my housekeeper/cook, Mr. Javier. The Cat Wars ended not long after my return home, with one side—the side opposite to mine—conceding defeat. Sadly, that came too late for my leg.

I'm sure you were surprised to learn that I am a doctor. Believe me, I understand. No one expects the cat to be a doctor. Humans, and other animals, believe wrongly that cats don't have enough focus to be professionals. And yet, a cat can spend more time focused on cleaning just one paw than an armadillo can spend deciding what to eat for lunch.

Yawn.

Some of us live more exciting lives than others

expect we will. My own family expected me to settle down with a mate and have kittens, and I still might someday. But I wanted something more exciting. I wanted the most I could dream of, outside of chasing rabbits, and so I studied to become a surgeon. Being in a war, though, that had been plenty enough excitement for me. I was glad to be home again at good old 221B Baker Street, the two-story row house I've lived in since I got my license to practice medicine. It's a row house, meaning that it shares side walls with other houses. I don't mind having neighbors so much, so long as I don't have to talk to them. I live mostly on the second story of my home, using the lower half for storage and things; also, the ground floor is where Mr. Javier's quarters are. Not only does it allow him his own private space, but it's also easier for him to get to the front door from there. Living on the upper story further allows me to keep more distance between myself and the rest of the world.

Now all I wanted was peace and quiet and to nap in my yard.

Only, I couldn't stop thinking about the friend who had stopped by the day before. Let's call him Paul. When Paul arrived, he had looked about awkwardly, clearly hoping I would invite him in for a treat or perhaps a go at playing soccer with my ball of yarn. But I had no such desire. I'm not much for entertaining.

Paul had then told me that he had a friend who was looking for a place to live and that, after my adventures, he thought it would be good for me to have some regular company. I snorted. The very idea! I know what comes with regular company: irregular naps, that's what. As soon as I was done snorting, Paul mentioned how he knew I had plenty of rooms in my house and that he thought his friend would like those rooms very much. Also, he was tired of having his friend lodge with him and had exhausted his supply of other friends upon whom he might fob off this one. He told me his friend's name—Sherlock Bones—and I couldn't help but immediately think what an odd one it was.

That's when I told my friend to be on his merry

way. I informed him that while I did not mind occasional company, I neither wanted nor needed regular company.

There, I thought, watching him go. Paul looked so glum, slouching away, his orange tail between his legs. *That's taken care of!*

Little did I know that I was about to learn just how wrong I was, and that, when it came to Sherlock Bones, nothing was ever easy.

CHAPTER TWO

Putting aside my thoughts of Paul's visit, I drifted off to sleep in my yard. I was enjoying the most lovely dream. In it, I was chasing rabbits—I would never *hurt* rabbits, mind you; I just like to *chase* them—when I heard the sound of loud panting in my ear.

Opening one eye, I saw a dog before me. But not just *any* dog. This dog was sitting back on hind legs, and, if I had to guess, I'd say it was a Great Dane wearing a deerstalker hat. *Odd choice of hat*, I thought, closing my eye again. I wasn't the slightest bit scared. In my experience, if I don't bother other creatures, they don't bother me. I figured if I just ignored it, it would go away.

But no.

"Dr. Catson, I presume?" the dog said.

This time, I opened both eyes.

"Who wants to know?" I asked warily.

"I am Sherlock Bones," the dog informed me.

That name sounded disturbingly familiar.

"I believe," the dog went on, "Our Mutual Friend said I would be stopping by?"

It took me a while to piece together what he was telling me. Yes, it had only been one day since Paul had come to call. But you must realize, I'd napped at least a dozen separate times since then. So for me, it felt like ages ago.

And then it hit me. Who this was. What this was about.

"He never said you were a dog!" I cried, outraged.

"And he never said you were a cat," the dog said. "But since he is one himself, I deduced that you were likely one as well."

"I told him," I said, "that I don't want a housemate."

7

"Yes, I believe he may have mentioned that small fact. But never mind that now, though, because— " And here, his eyes grew wide in excitement as he raised a paw in the air as though pointing at the sky. "The game's afoot!"

"Which one?" I yawned.

"Pardon?"

"Well, you have four feet, don't you? So I want to know: Which foot are we talking about?"

"That's not what I meant!"

"Then why on earth did you say it?"

I might have been wrong, but it did seem to me that the dog was starting to look annoyed.

"What I meant was," the dog said, a gleam of excitement filling his eyes again, "a crime has been committed!"

CHAPTER THREE

"By whom?" I asked.

"Some humans."

"That's nothing new." *Yawn*. "Human are always committing one crime or another."

"Yes, but this time — "

I rose and stretched each of my front paws out one at a time, and then I arched my back to its fullest height as I turned away from him—ahh!—which immediately served to cut him off. It's amazing how turning your back on someone can have that effect. Then, I began to walk away.

"You're limping," he called after me.

"How observant of you," I said. "Yes, I was wounded in the Cat Wars."

"I've heard of those!" He seemed pleased to know this. "I heard you creatures fought like cats and … "

I stopped him with a steely glare. "You were going to say 'cats and dogs,' weren't you?" I said.

"*No*." He seemed equally embarrassed and offended. "I was going to say … 'cats and cats'! But never mind that now. I am so very sorry you were hurt. My good chap— "

"I'm not a chap."

"Pardon?"

"I'm a girl."

"Pardon?"

"I'm a *lady*!"

"Oh. Oh!"

"I'm Dr. Jane Catson. People are always thinking it's *John*, but it's *Jane*."

Just like no one ever expects the cat to be a doctor, no one ever expects the cat doctor to be a female. Well, just because no one expects it, it doesn't mean it's impossible.

"Yes, well, as I was saying," he went on. "About the crime ... "

Turning away from him once more, I proceeded toward the house.

"Come along, Bones," I invited.

"Actually, I prefer Sherlock, Jane."

"And I prefer 'Doctor' or 'Catson.' Come along then, Bones."

I could tell he wasn't going to leave until I'd listened to his story and, frankly, I did not want him to tell it to me on my front lawn where all the world—at least the neighborhood—could see.

After all, he was a dog.

What would the neighbors think?

CHAPTER FOUR

As we walked up to my front door, the dog glanced up at the house number and remarked, "Ah, 221B—what a perfect address!"

"I've always thought so," I said dryly, then I reached out one paw to push in the small rectangle of my own personal entrance. I was about to step inside when I heard the dog cry out, "I'll never fit through there!" Then I heard him mutter, "When I move in, we shall have to install a bigger flap for me."

"You won't be staying around long enough for that," I said, pulling my hind legs through. Then I turned to poke my head back out through my flap.

"You're a big boy," I told him. "Reach up to the handle and use the regular door."

He had some trouble with the doorknob—those great big clumsy paws of his—but once he was inside, I led him up the long flight of hardwood stairs, the center of which is lined with an Oriental carpet runner, to what I like to think of as my apartments. Even though I own the whole row house, since Mr. Javier lives on the first floor, it's cozier for me to think of the rooms on the second floor as my apartments.

"How cozy," he said, taking in the overstuffed sofa and side chairs, the roaring fire in the stone fireplace, the multiple scratching posts and the cushion in front of the bay window overlooking the road.

I sincerely hoped he wasn't going to go about pawing at all my things, picking up framed pictures and such as guests are sometimes inclined to do.

Instead he sat back, raised his front paws into fists and took fast jabs at the air in front of him. Then he nearly rose up on his hind legs and, with his left paw on his left hip, used his right paw to make big sweeping motions.

13

"What *are* you doing?" I demanded.

"Seeing if there's sufficient room in here for boxing and swordplay, two of my many hobbies. I do believe there is."

"Please," I said, "don't make yourself at home."

He seemed startled at my rudeness. But what could I say? I certainly wasn't about to encourage him.

"221B," he said again, stroking his chin, "on Baker Street. When we entered, I believe I saw a rabbit hanging the wash out of the window next door. Is that something new? Didn't Baker Street used to be part of the Cats-Only Quarter?"

"Yes, it is relatively new, if you call twenty years ago new, which was before both of our times; and yes, it used to be. Once it became widely understood and accepted that animals could speak – such a shock to humans when *that* happened!—the city was divided into quarters: the Cat Quarter, the Dog Quarter, the Human Quarter, and the Everything-Else Quarter. But then, eventually, the walls came down. London became one big melting pot although the species still don't have much tolerance for one another, the humans being the worst of the bunch. But surely, you must know all that."

"Of course I do. I merely wanted to see if you were up on your history. So many ignore the teachings of the past, much to their own harm."

Oh, great. Now he was wasting my time, getting me to tell him things he already knew.

"You mentioned something about a crime?" I prompted.

"That's correct. I am, as Our Mutual Friend may have informed you, a consulting detective."

"Our Mutual Friend never said anything about that."

"Yes, well, from time to time, people come to me with—" He stopped speaking as his long nose began to twitch. "Tomato?" he asked, pronouncing it wrong.

I nodded.

"Garlic?"

I nodded again.

"*Turtle*?" he asked, looking puzzled this time.

I must confess, his sense of observation was impressive. Well, his nose's was at any rate.

"Yes." I nodded a third time. "*That* would be Mr. Javier."

I turned and led us through a doorway into my well-equipped kitchen, Bones's nose quivering and sniffing the whole way. I worried that next, he'd be drooling. Well, it did smell good.

We watched as Mr. Javier, his white apron tied securely behind his shell and his chef's toque perched jauntily over one of his black eyes, carefully used a wooden spoon to stir the large boiling pots of pasta and sauce on the stove.

"That's Mr. Javier," I said. "He's making lunch."

"How extraordinary!" Bones said, observing the turtle. "Our Mutual Friend said you were intelligent, almost as intelligent as me—"

"*Almost as intelligent a—*"

"But I never dreamt … " In an apparent state of awe, Bones approached the turtle, who—at this point—had stopped stirring his pasta in the pot and was now starting his slow, inching journey toward the canister of oregano. I do like a lot of oregano in my tomato sauce. Without asking permission, Bones picked up the turtle and turned him over, studying the underside closely as Mr. Javier's tiny chef's toque fell to the ground and his scaly little reptile legs waved helplessly in the air.

"But I don't understand," Bones said, clearly puzzled. Then he glanced up at me. "Where is the mechanism?"

"The mechanism for what?"

"This is a robot, isn't it? A robot you've designed yourself?"

"I'm not a robot!" Mr. Javier cried in his native Castilian accent, speaking to Bones for the first time. I'd never seen Mr. Javier so outraged before, and frankly, I was outraged on his behalf.

"He's not a robot!" I informed Bones. "He's *real*! He's a turtle, not to mention, my housekeeper and chef. Did I not say: '*That's Mr. Javier!*'?"

The dog, still holding Mr. Javier, looked equal parts fascinated and dumbfounded.

CHAPTER FIVE

"Oh, I see!" Bones set Mr. Javier back on the counter. "Yes, well, but wouldn't he be more efficient with a jetpack?"

"A *what*?"

"A jetpack. You know, a pack worn on the back and propelled by jets so that one can move more speedily from place to place?"

"I *know* what a jetpack is!" Actually, I had never heard of one before, but this dog did have a way of getting under my skin.

"Of course you didn't know what a jetpack was before I told you," he said. "You didn't know because they don't exist yet. But I shall rectify that by inventing one this very day."

"Whatever," I fumed. "What I don't know is why Mr. Javier would want one."

Bones immediately cast a meaningful gaze upon Mr. Javier, who had only progressed a few short inches toward the oregano while we were speaking. The oregano, which I should mention, was still a good two feet away. Lunch, I feared, would be late again.

"Actually, Boss," Mr. Javier admitted with a glance over his shoulder toward me, "I don't think I'd mind my own jetpack. Sometimes, just doing the marketing can take me several days."

"Fine," I sighed. "But where am I supposed to find a jetpack small enough—"

I trailed off as the dog raised one paw in the air in what was quickly becoming a familiar gesture, a silly struck-by-lightning look upon his face. "Did you not hear me before? I shall invent one!"

"Of course you shall." I yawned as I began to exit the room.

19

"Where are you going?" Bones called after me. "I was about to tell you about the crime that's been committed!"

"Mr. Javier," I said, ignoring Bones, "throw in some more pasta and add another place setting at the table. It looks like there'll be one more for lunch today."

"But where are you going?" Bones demanded.

"To take my nap."

"Didn't you just take one?"

"I take lots of naps." After my time in the Cat Wars, I needed even more rest than I once did. "You'll get used to it. Or rather, I should say, please don't get used to it. Oh, but while you are here?"

"Yes?"

"Take *off* that ridiculous hat. You're in the house!"

As I curled up on my favorite place to nap inside the house, the floral cushion in the bay window that catches the afternoon sun and looks out upon the street, I thought about how, thus far, I was not hugely impressed with the dog. But in an hour, all of that would change.

CHAPTER SIX

In my dream, Mr. Javier was flying, and then a voice was calling, "Lunch is ready, Boss!"

Only it wasn't a dream.

As I opened one eye, I looked up to see Mr. Javier, his back bumping up against the high ceiling. There was something wrapped around his waist that wasn't his usual chef's apron. Also, somehow he'd got his chef's toque back.

I heard a loud, "Ahem!" and looked over to see the dog. Around him on the floor were scattered tools and fabric.

"You're still here," I observed.

"Yes."

"And you made Mr. Javier a jetpack while I was sleeping, didn't you?"

"Yes."

"Lunch is ready, Boss," said Mr. Javier. "Only I can't figure out how to get down from here."

"The turtle is finding it to be a little bit of a learning curve," the dog said. "But don't worry, he's very bright. I'm sure he'll get the hang of it … eventually."

One could hope. Particularly since one was hungry.

A short time, and a brief panic spell on the part of the turtle, later, Mr. Javier was down from the ceiling and luncheon was served. We ate, of course, in the dining room. It has a formal table with high-backed chairs and a tall ceiling. I like a tall ceiling. The fine china had been set out (although if I'd been asked, I could have told Mr. Javier that it was probably wasted on the dog). The oregano-spiced sauce smelled heavenly.

"Don't worry, Mr. Javier," I said. "I can serve. You've done quite enough for one day."

Naturally, I had to tell the dog to take his elbows off the table.

Once I'd piled pasta and sauce on our respective plates, he dove right in, sauce flying everywhere as he shoveled pasta into his mouth. Honestly, some creatures. He was almost as bad as a human.

After a moment, he must have sensed my eyes upon him and looked up.

"What is it?" he said. "Do I have sauce all over my face?"

"I thought," I said dryly, "that you were eager to tell me about whatever is 'a foot'." I paused. "You know, *your case*?"

CHAPTER SEVEN

"Well," Bones said, "technically, a crime hasn't been committed yet. But one will be."

"How do you know that?"

"Wasn't it you who said there always is some crime or another being committed by humans? And then, I believe, you yawned."

That did sound like me. "And just what sort of crime are you expecting?"

"If I had to guess?"

I nodded.

"A murder."

Not exactly what I was expecting. If *I* had to

guess, I'd have gone with some petty crime, like shoplifting something tasty for dinner or sneaking out of a restaurant without paying the bill first. But *murder*? That seemed a little farfetched.

"*Murder?*" I said, voicing my doubt out loud.

"Oh, yes," he said as though it were nothing. "It's what I'm most frequently consulted about."

Before I could ask him what he meant, the doorbell rang.

"Isn't the turtle going to get that?" he asked.

"The turtle's name is Mr. Javier," I said, annoyed. I may have referred to Mr. Javier as the turtle often, but I rather resented the dog doing so. As the bell continued to ring, I looked through to the living room where I saw the turtle passed out on the large Turkish area rug, the jetpack still on his back. "And no, I don't think so. I believe Mr. Javier has exhausted himself."

I picked up my fork again. "Anyway," I said, "I wasn't expecting anybody."

"It's probably for me," the dog said, rising.

"For *you*? Why would my doorbell ringing be *for you?*"

"Because I left this as my forwarding address when I moved, didn't I?" he said mildly, moving to the staircase.

"What?" I shouted, racing after him down the stairs. "You don't even live here!"

"Well," he said, his voice still mild, "I did tell you I was a detective, didn't I?"

Of course he had. But I hadn't believed him.

"I'm a consulting detective," he said. "People come to me for my opinion when they've lost all hope. They've been coming to me ever since I solved my first case involving rampant chew-toy theft when I was just a puppy, followed soon after by a criminal case I solved involving humans; that time, the butler did *not* do it. Do you not read the newspapers?"

He paused, waiting for my response. What? Did he expect me to be impressed? Surely, he was making all this nonsense up, and so I merely stared back at him.

"Naturally, people need some address to come to for my consultation," he continued when I failed to respond in the admiring way he no doubt would have liked me to. "I mean, it wouldn't look very professional to just meet with clients on any street corner, would it?" He paused. "And the thing they come to consult with me most about?" He didn't wait for my answer. "Murder."

It occurred to me for the first time: the dog was delusional.

Before I could say as much, he flung open *my* front door.

On the stoop was a human.

It was your basic garden-variety model: a pair of legs attached to a body, a head slapped on top.

"Are you Sherlock Bones?" the human asked the dog.

"I am," Bones said proudly.

"Telegram for you." The human handed Bones a piece of paper. "There's been a murder."

Well, blow me down.

CHAPTER EIGHT

But I wasn't blown down for long.

As Bones closed the door and headed back up the stairs, I shouted after him, "That was probably all a setup!"

"How so?" Bones said once we were back in the living room.

Before I could respond, the dog lay down on the hardwood part of my living room floor and began rolling back and forth energetically.

"What *are* you doing?" I demanded.

"Sorry," he said, still rolling, as though he neither could nor wished to control himself. In fact, he didn't sound sorry at all. "But I need to do this a few times a day. You have your naps; for me, it's all about a quick roll on the floor. Plus, it just feels good."

"That man," I said, trying not to be distracted by all the annoying rolling. "You must have, I don't know, paid him off to come here and give you that piece of paper."

The dog, at last, stopped rolling and rose to his feet. "Any why would I do that?"

"Because, for some reason, you want me to believe you're a detective." I paused. "Which you're not."

"Oh, but I am."

"Then prove it," I said.

"And how shall I do that?"

"I don't know. You're the detective. Do something … *detective-y*."

"Very well. That man who was just here?"

I nodded.

"He had a lot of eggs for breakfast this morning, but he's still hungry. He also lives at home with his mother."

"How do you know all that?"

"The profusion of yellow specks on his shirt. The fact that his stomach was growling. Oh, and the tie."

"The tie?"

"Yes. No grown man would pick out such a hideous tie for himself. Had to be the mother."

Huh.

"I didn't notice any of those things," I said, disbelievingly.

"How could you not have?" the dog said. "They were pretty obvious."

"OK," I granted, "so maybe you're a little more observant than I gave you credit for—"

"The china we ate our lunch on," he continued. "It was your best china, even though you never said so. You took too much care with it for it to be something you use every day. The oregano was stale. You really should use fresh if you can get it. Absent that, you should buy smaller bottles. You know, spices do lose something if left on the shelf too long."

I was about to point out that Mr. Javier always

buys in bulk to save on trips he has to make to the market, but Bones cut me off with, "And that turtle." At this point, I was too stunned by him to point out that the turtle had a name. "He's one hundred and forty-seven years old."

"How on earth did you know that?"

"Turtles have growth rings," he said, as if everyone should know this. "They're like trees in that, you know. Just count the growth rings on a turtle or a tree and you have the age." He paused. "Plus, I asked him while you were napping."

"HAH!" I may have been HAH!-ing at him, but in truth, I was astounded. I never would have guessed Mr. Javier was so old. Also, I'm embarrassed to admit, it had never occurred to me to ask him.

"And when you're annoyed with me," he said, pointing a paw at my face as he squinted one eye, "you squint your right eye just a little bit. It's always the right eye, never the left."

"I do not—" I started to object but then stopped myself as I felt my right eye starting to squint. "Still," I said, "that's not very much."

"It's enough. It's more than most creatures or humans can claim. I can identify thousands of items by smell. I can remember every face I've ever seen, however briefly. I have an encyclopedic knowledge of all sorts of subjects." He glanced at the telegram again. "And now I know that a fresh murder has been committed."

Then he crumpled up the telegram and tossed it aside.

"I also know," Bones said, "that I'm not going to bother trying to solve it."

What?

CHAPTER NINE

"You can't be serious!" I practically shouted, outraged.

If a murder really had been committed, I couldn't believe he wasn't going to do anything about it. I also couldn't believe that I was arguing with him about this. I'd never wanted to get involved with him and all his craziness in the first place.

"Oh, but I am, my dear Catson."

My dear ... Who did this dog think he was?

"And why is that, *Bones*?" I demanded, determined not to let my right eye squint.

"Because I am tired of not getting credit."

"What *are* you talking about?"

"Here's how this kind of case always goes: a crime, usually murder, occurs. The professional, public detectives—the so-called 'experts'—are called in. They fail to solve the case. Then I am called in. I solve the case, but they take all the credit. End of story."

As he spoke, his eyes shifted sadly from me to the floor to studying his toenails.

I found myself, for the first time, starting to feel sorry for him. Then:

"Wait," I said, this time letting my right eye go ahead and twitch. "You're not going to investigate, you're going to let a murderer run free—*because your feelings are hurt?* Because you feel you don't get enough *credit?*"

"Well," he said, now looking slightly embarrassed, "yes, that is exactly what I plan to do. Or rather, not do."

"You can't be serious! If you think you can help, it is your duty to do so!"

"I suppose … " His eyes met mine. "Do you

want to come with?"

"Come with where?"

He eagerly un-crumpled the crumpled piece of paper.

"There," he said, pointing to an address.

I thought of my lunch, which was still sitting on the table. I thought longingly of the cushion in front of the bay window, my nap long overdue. And then I thought of the adventure of potentially aiding to solve a murder. I must confess: I was curious. It also occurred to me that perhaps since returning home from the Cat Wars, my life had been a little dull.

"*Fine*," I said, mildly exasperated with myself.

"Great," he said, all smiles once more. "I'll go get my hat."

CHAPTER TEN

"Must you wear that?" I said, staring at the ridiculous hat on the equally ridiculous Great Dane striding beside me on the pavement. He had been striding so quickly on his long legs since we left Baker Street that I had to scamper to keep up.

"Yes," he said mildly, "I must. When I'm on a case, it helps me think. Chewing on bones also helps me think; however, I noticed you had none available. We shall have to ask Mr. Javier to add some to our shopping list."

"*Our* shopping … but you don't live there!"

There was no point, though, in arguing with him further at the moment because …

"This is the place!" Bones announced, as though he'd just made some great discovery.

I glanced at the building in question. It was a large multi-story house that looked like it hadn't been lived in, in quite some time. I could tell by the rundown look of everything and the overgrown little patch of grass out front. There were also a few broken windows on the top story. Human beings are nowhere near as tidy as cats, but even they won't let a broken window sit unrepaired.

The front door was a few inches open.

Immediately, the dog began sniffing around the ground outside the door and muttering to himself.

"Two different sets of footprints … they must have come here in a cab … the cab left them off here …"

By *cab*, of course he meant one of those vehicles pulled by horses. I never use them. In my experience, horses are not very good conversationalists.

"Right," he announced.

"Right what?" I said.

"Shall we go inside?" Bones asked, his paw inches from the open door.

"Shouldn't we wait?" I said.

"For what?"

"I don't know." Usually, an open door is such an inviting thing. But sometimes, an open door can appear menacing. This was definitely one of the latter. "Perhaps it's dangerous?"

"I hardly think so." Bones snorted. "Whomever was killed is already dead. How much can he hurt us now?"

CHAPTER ELEVEN

No sooner had we stepped through the front door than there came the sound of loud voices from the back of the house. I wouldn't say they were necessarily shouting, but they were most definitely human, which almost always means loud.

I was about to suggest we just leave, but after placing a paw to his muzzle to indicate he wished us to remain silent, Bones proceeded to tiptoe toward the source of the voices. Well, as capably as a Great Dane can tiptoe. Once again, it was all I could do to follow. Of course, it was easier for me to tread silently, even with my permanent limp. Cats are, after all, better suited to quiet walking than dogs.

The voices, increasing in volume as we tiptoed, led us to a room at the back of the house. It was a very dusty room—frankly, the whole place was dusty—and inside of it were two humans, their backs to us. Their heads were tilted slightly downward as though studying some object on the threadbare carpet before them. They were talking so loudly that they hadn't even heard our approach. Neither did they look up as Bones began to whisper to me.

"The one on the right," Bones informed me, "is Inspector Strange. He's with the police. If I'm a more private detective, then he's a very public one. And not a very good one, I might add, which is why he always calls for my help. But as I mentioned before, when I give it and solve the case, he then always goes and takes all the credit."

"And why would he do that?"

"Human nature?" Bones shrugged. "Also, I suspect he has a prejudice against dogs. He accepts that animals can talk and live amongst his kind independently, but he doesn't like to think that a dog can actually outsmart a human."

A prejudice against dogs? I thought sarcastically. *Why would anyone ever feel that?* I'd never had anything in common with humans before but I suppose there's always a first for everything. Unless there never is.

"Who's the other one?" I asked. "The man on the left?"

"Another detective, but he's no one very important." He paused. "Ahem!" Bones uttered loudly, causing the two men to turn where they stood.

"Ah, Bones!" Inspector Strange said, his face a peculiar mixture of pleased and not pleased. I say peculiar, yet I could fully relate to it. Already, in our short acquaintance, Bones had the same *peculiar* effect on me.

Rather than return the greeting, Bones commenced to slapping at the area behind his ears with his great big paws.

"Sorry," he said, for once looking slightly embarrassed. "Fleas."

Fleas? And he'd been in my *house?*

"I'm glad you decided to join us," Inspector Strange continued. "And who have you brought with you?"

"This is my partner," Bones informed him, "Dr. Catson."

Partner? I never agreed to be his *partner!*

But before I could object to this classification, Inspector Strange held out a hand awkwardly as though trying to figure out what part of my body he could politely shake.

I saved him the trouble as I reached up one elegant paw and shook his hand firmly. My father always said a firm handshake shows good character.

"Pleased to meet you," Inspector Strange said, "my good chap."

"I'm not a chap," I said. "I'm a lady."

"Sorry!" Inspector Strange said, blushing. "But you can understand my error, can't you? I mean, it's always so much easier to tell with dogs."

What an idiot! I thought, and *Bones is right—he's not much of a detective!*

Of course, Bones hadn't been able to ascertain my gender on initial meeting either, but that's about what you'd expect from a dog.

Since no one else was going to introduce us, I offered my paw to the other detective. "Hello. Dr. Jane Catson here."

But since no one gave him a name, and he didn't provide one himself, I began to think of him just as Bones had described him: as Inspector No One Very Important.

Once my paw had been limply shaken and then released by Inspector No One Very Important, the two public detectives returned to contemplating the object on the carpet before them, turning their backs on us once more. Only this time, there was separation between the two public detectives' bodies so that we could get a glimpse at what they were looking at.

"Well, what do you think, Bones?" Inspector Strange asked.

It was a human body, facedown, and quite obviously dead.

You never do forget your first, do you?

CHAPTER TWELVE

When I say it was my first, I don't mean it was my first dead creature. In the Cat Wars, I'd seen far too many. But I'd never seen a dead body like this. This dead body hadn't been killed in conflict or as the natural result of being part of the food chain. This body had been *murdered*.

As I said, it was my first. And as such, completely unforgettable. In fact, it was so startling, I couldn't look away from it, couldn't take in anything else in the room.

Murder—it's just wrong, somehow.

I wanted to run as far away from it as possible.

I also wanted desperately to find out what had happened to cause it to be in this state. And I also really, *really* wanted my nap. *So* overdue.

"Well, what do you think, Bones?" Inspector Strange repeated.

"What do *you* think, Dr. Catson?" Bones asked, turning to me and causing the others to turn to me as well.

Me?

"Well, he's dead, of course," I said.

The others continued to look at me.

"Well, come on." I pointed at the corpse before us. "Just look at the man! I mean, he's really, *really* dead."

Still, they waited.

"I don't think it's possible for a man to be deader than *that*," I said.

I could be wrong, but I think all three rolled their eyes at me.

"Yes, that part is obvious," Bones said. "But what can you tell us about the murder?"

Now that my initial shock was lessening, I found I could think more clearly. Tilting my head, I considered the body.

I may have mentioned that I don't pay too much attention to humans. As far as I'm concerned, they're all just stick figures with round heads attached at the top. But if this was a murder investigation, and I was meant to help, I supposed I should at least take notice of what the dead chap looked like.

He looked to be in his forties, as human ages go. He was medium in most ways, but had wide shoulders and dark hair—on his head, of course. He had a suit on, so for all I knew his shoulders could have been hairy too. He also had a close-cropped beard. And was very, *very* dead.

I tilted my head to the other side, considering something else.

"But how do we know it *was* a murder?" I asked.

"Excuse me?" Bones said.

"There's no blood, no obvious wounds, no signs whatsoever of a struggle. I mean, couldn't he have just died there right where he was? Like that?"

"Because death doesn't happen like that!" Bones said.

It doesn't? I thought. One time, I knocked a goldfish bowl over, and the fish died where he was, *exactly* like that.

Having apparently decided that I was of limited use, at least for the time being, Inspector Strange turned to Bones once more.

"Well?" he said.

"There's what looks to be blood over there," Bones said, pointing toward a space on the carpet several feet away from the body, which he now nudged until it was lying on its back. It looked even worse in this position. "And yet there is not a single drop on the body itself. So, not shot, not stabbed, not a whole lot of other things. Not strangled either. See? There are no marks on his neck."

"*What* then?" Inspector Strange demanded, as though growing impatient with the dog. "Is it possible that your furry little companion is right?"

His furry little *what?*

"Is it possible," Inspector Strange pressed, "that this man wasn't murdered at all?"

"Of course not," Bones said. "He was murdered."

And then, before the dog could say it, I said it myself:

"He was poisoned."

CHAPTER THIRTEEN

"*P*oisoned?"

The two public detectives spoke the word at the same time as they turned to stare at me.

"Of course," I said, wrinkling my nose at the smell. "Don't you detect the scent of almonds around the body?"

Bones sniffed the air and then nodded in agreement. The public detectives sniffed the air but then only looked puzzled.

"Yes," I said, "almonds. And unless this man had some kind of bizarre almond habit, I'd say he was given cyanide. One of the characteristics of cyanide poisoning is the scent of almonds. The foaming at the mouth is a bit of a dead giveaway too."

"I knew I was right to select you as my partner," Bones said, and it was impossible to tell from his smile whether he was more pleased with me or with himself.

I was about to object to his words—*he* selected *me*? and, "partner" again?—when he added, "You know, we two are somewhat alike in our strengths, are we not? For what is a great doctor—a surgeon, no less!—but a detective of the human body. You are presented with mysteries of a medical nature, and you solve them."

Despite my reservations where the dog was concerned, I couldn't help but be flattered at this. My own family had never recognized my strengths so accurately.

"What can you tell me about the victim?" Bones asked Inspector Strange. "Have you identified the body?"

"Well, it's a man," Inspector Strange started.

Now it was my turn to roll my eyes.

"Yes, but a name would be a better place to start," Bones said. "If you don't have one, I'm sure I can find out."

"No, that's quite all right," Inspector Strange said. "He had I.D. in his back pocket."

"And?" Bones prompted.

Inspector Strange said the name. It was one of those particularly confusing human names, a German one from the sound of it, Something Drebber or Drebber Something, I forget which.

"Everyone OK if we just refer to him as John Smith from here on in?" I interrupted.

The others looked surprised but then shrugged. At least no one objected. Well, *I* thought it was a good suggestion.

"After you found the identifying papers," Bones asked, "did you look in any of, er, *John Smith's* other pockets?"

Inspector Strange and Inspector No One Very Important looked dumbfounded.

"Perhaps," Bones prompted, "you'd care to do so now?"

"Oh. Right!" Inspector Strange said. He pointed toward the body, indicating that Inspector No One Very Important should do the search. Good. If the man wasn't going to talk, he might as well contribute by doing something useful.

Inspector No One Very Important's search of the remaining pockets yielded a half-empty pack of gum, a torn stub from the theater, a wallet that still had plenty of cash in it—causing Bones to conclude that the motive was *not* robbery—and lots of lint. Oh, and also a document indicating that John Smith had been traveling in the country with his secretary, some other man whose name I didn't immediately get. I was about to suggest that we just call this other man John Smith, but then realized how that might get confusing.

"Curiouser and curiouser," Bones said. "He also has two letters—one addressed to him and one to the secretary—and some jewelry, a book with the secretary's name in it, and tickets home to his own country."

"I agree," I said, "that is all curious—not to

mention, the man has some very crowded pockets. Does the theatre stub say which performance he saw?"

"Yes," Bones said, considering, "but that's neither here nor there. After all, we do have a motive."

"We *do?*"

The three of us regarded the dog.

"Or, at least, the murderer wants us to *think* it's the motive." Bones shrugged. "It's revenge."

"*How,*" I said, "do you know *that?*"

What *was* the dog talking about?

"I know it because it says it right there." Bones pointed at the far wall. "Don't you see? It's written on the wall, plain as day."

CHAPTER FOURTEEN

"Well, it doesn't say 'REVENGE' exactly," the dog amended, regarding the letters, which were indeed written in dripping red.

How *had* we all missed that?

Was that *blood*?

I went over to the wall and sniffed, but my sniffing did not detect the metallic scent of blood I'd learned to know all too well during the Cat Wars. This was mere paint, as the stain on the carpet turned out to be as well, once I went over and sniffed at that too.

"Too right," Inspector Strange said. "It says 'RACHE.' Probably, the victim, this, er, *John Smith* didn't have time to write the whole name, which would have undoubtedly been RACHEL, a woman's name."

"But see, that's where you're wrong!" Bones said. "That's just what someone else *wants* you to think! Someone is relying on some stupid flatfoot to go barking up the wrong tree—always a waste of time, no matter how pleasurable—and turning over every stone in town to find the right Rachel."

"Right," Inspector Strange said, blushing. "What a silly thing it would be, to do that." Pause. "And why would that be exactly?"

"Because it's not referring to a woman's name at all," Bones said. "RACHE is the German word for REVENGE."

"Ah!" Inspector Strange said. "Helpful, is it? Being multilingual like that?"

"It comes in handy," Bones allowed.

"But wait," Inspector Strange said. "You're saying it was someone other than the victim who left that note on the wall?"

Bones nodded.

"Why would someone do that, though?" Inspector Strange said. "No, I'm sure it would have been the victim. You know, trying to tell us that's why he was killed?"

"Do you not remember," Bones said, "that the victim had no red on him, no marks at all? And this word written in red—it was, I am quite certain, written with a human finger. And yet the victim has no red on his hands."

"Oh. Right." Inspector Strange appeared stumped. "Then who … ? Why … ?"

"That, my good Inspector, is what is known as a mystery."

CHAPTER
FIFTEEN

Then, Bones did an astonishing thing. Based on observations I could barely understand or follow, he somehow gave a full physical description of the murderer along with details about the mode of transportation the murderer had used to get to the scene of the crime. He made these deductions, he said, based on evidence he'd seen outside the abandoned house as well as evidence on the dusty floors inside—length of stride and its relationship to height, followed by a whole bunch of other things. Then he mentioned a cab, as he had to me earlier, and said something about two men arriving as friends but not remaining so.

"I wonder what happened?" he mused, paw to lip, considering.

I suppose I could have paid more attention, but I was very hungry. Not to mention that the body was still right there, and I was so far overdue for my nap I couldn't think straight.

"Didn't anyone else notice this?" Bones said, shifting the body a bit more to uncover a bright, shiny object.

I must confess, I've been known to get distracted by bright, shiny objects. By squirrels, too.

"What's that?" Inspector Strange asked.

"Obviously," Bones said, "it's a woman's gold wedding ring. You can tell it's a woman's from the size of the ring hole." He held it up to one eye, peering at us through the hole, showing us it was a simple gold band with no further adornment.

"Great," I said. "So a woman was here too."

"Not necessarily," Bones said. "Just because a woman's ring is here, it doesn't necessarily follow that the woman was."

"Right," I said. "Now that that's settled, I think I'll go home for my nap."

"Not so fast," Bones said. "I need you to come with me."

"Not another dead body," I groaned.

"Of course not," Bones said, which he quickly amended to, "at least, I hope not." He turned to Inspector Strange. "Can you tell me the name of the person who first discovered, er, John Smith?"

Inspector Strange named some constable, a constable being what your basic police officers are called in this part of the world. But honestly, at this point, in my sleep-deprived state, it was just gibberish to me.

"Come along, Catson," Bones said with an annoying level of energy.

"Where are we going now?" I grumbled.

"To see Gibberish, of course," Bones said.

Did he really say that, or did I just imagine it?

CHAPTER SIXTEEN

We found Constable Gibberish at home.

He was even less helpful than one would imagine a man named Gibberish might be.

He was also wearing a tasseled sleeping cap and striped nightshirt and rubbing his eyes when he answered the door.

"I'm sorry," Bones said. "Did we wake you?"

"Yes, but that's all right. I tend to sleep during the daytime."

Don't we all, I thought, stifling a yawn.

"I am Sherlock Bones," Bones began.

"I know who you are, sir," Gibberish said.

He *did*? And "sir?"

"Everyone knows who Sherlock Bones is, sir," said Gibberish.

They *did*? *Everyone*? I'd never heard of him before today. *Huh*. Perhaps I did need to pay more attention to the newspapers?

"And this is my partner, Dr. Catson," Bones continued.

Partner. There was that annoying word again! I was about to correct Bones when he continued with, "And we are here to question you about, er, John Smith."

"Who?" Gibberish said.

"The dead body you found in the abandoned house earlier today?"

"Oh. Him." Gibberish was puzzled. "But I thought his name was … " And here he said the complicated German name.

"Yes, well," Bones said, "we're all calling him, er, John Smith now."

"Huh." Gibberish scratched his head. "I'm not sure what I can tell you. What is it you want to know?"

"For starters, how did you discover him?"

"I was just passing by, making my rounds, wasn't I?"

"I don't know. You tell me. *Were* you?"

Gibberish appeared startled at this. "Yes, I just said, didn't I?"

"Actually, your words contained an upwards inflection at the end, as though you were posing a question, so I thought perhaps you were asking *me*."

Once again, Gibberish appeared puzzled. All I could think was, *Oh, Bones. Must you try to word play with him? Can't you see he's just a simple man?*

"At any rate," Gibberish said, "I was passing by, saw the door was open, and thought it looked suspicious. So, I went inside, found the dead body, phoned it in, waited for the inspectors to arrive, and that was it."

"That was *it*?" Bones was incredulous.

"I'm not sure what more you want me to say. The inspectors arrived, and I came back here and immediately laid down for a nap. I was that tired."

"But didn't you see anything else worth mentioning?" Bones pressed.

Gibberish appeared to consider this, then shook his head. "Nope."

"Really?" Bones pressed some more.

More considering, more head shaking. "Nope."

"Really?" Bones simply would not let this go. "Nothing? Nothing at all? Nothing in the least way suspicious?"

Not even a consideration or a shake this time. "No." Pause. "Well, unless you include the man who tried to gain entry while I was guarding the door…"

"The man who…" Bones echoed.

"What man?" I said, unable to contain myself. Was this Gibberish an idiot? Did he not see where this might be important?

"He wasn't anybody." Gibberish waved his hand dismissively. "He was just some confused person stumbling about. He came to the wrong door, thought it was his. So I sent him on his merry way. That's all."

"That's *all*?" Bones was incredulous. "Tell me, what did this harmless man look like?"

Gibberish considered then held up his hand about six feet from the ground. "He was about this tall and he smelled funny."

"Nothing else?" Bones pressed.

"Oh!" Gibberish said. "Almost forgot. He had the tiniest feet for such a tall man."

Bones looked at me, his eyes filled with meaning. He stared at me so long, I became uncomfortable. "What?" I finally said.

"Do you not see, Catson?"

"See what? If I could, would I be asking you?"

"Back at the abandoned house?" Bones prompted.

I thought about it, shook my head. "Still got nothing here."

"I gave a description to Inspector Strange of what my deductions led me to believe the murderer looked like."

"And?" I said.

Bones was clearly having trouble containing himself. "And it exactly fits the person Gibberish has just described!"

"You mean … " Gibberish couldn't bring himself to complete the sentence.

"Yes, Gibberish," Bones said. "You were the only person to see the murderer—and you sent the murderer on his merry way."

CHAPTER SEVENTEEN

"What does this mean?" I asked Bones.

We were back on the street again, having left Gibberish behind to return to his nap.

"Isn't it the usual order of things," I went on, "for murderers to flee the scene of the crime?"

"Yes, it is," Bones agreed.

"It doesn't make sense," I said. "Why would this murderer go *toward* the scene?"

"Because he forgot something."

"That makes no sense either. What could he have forgotten? He certainly didn't forget to kill his victim. We saw the body. We know he remembered to do that part."

"Forgotten. Lost. Pick any word you like. What it boils down to is that he left behind something at the scene, and he wanted it back."

I stopped walking and stared at the dog. "Oh, right. And now I suppose you're going to tell me what that something is?"

"Of course. The woman's wedding ring."

"The … Oh. *Oh*."

"Come along, Catson, no time to dawdle."

"Where are we going?" I hurried to catch up.

"Back to our place."

I was about to correct him—there was no *our* place; there was only *my* place—but then a happy thought crossed my mind.

"You mean it's time for a nap?" I said, relieved.

"Don't be daft!" Bones barked a laugh.

"Then what? What are we going back to *my* place for?"

"We need," Bones announced self-importantly, "to send a few telegrams."

CHAPTER EIGHTEEN

On the way home, Bones became distracted by some chew toys in a shop window. His tongue hung out at the sight.

"Come along, Bones," I prodded him away, only to be stopped myself by an attractive display of yarn in the window of a crafts store. I do appreciate a good skein of yarn.

"Come along, Catson," he said, his turn to prod.

And so we continued, with only a few more stops at shop windows, until we arrived at my front door.

I was about to ask about those telegrams, but no sooner did I leap through my door than I smelled the most wonderful aroma coming from upstairs. Following my nose, I raced to the kitchen to find Mr. Javier stirring something at the stove.

"What *are* you cooking, Mr. Javier?" I asked. "It smells delicious."

"Salmon croquettes!" Mr. Javier said proudly, still wearing his jetpack. Only now, he had his chef's apron tied over it. "Normally, I'd never attempt such a complicated dish. Going to the fish monger's *and* the grocery on the same day? Too far. It would take me a week! But with this?" He pointed at the jetpack on his back. "I made it there and back again so quickly, I even had time for my programs."

Mr. Javier does like his soap operas on the radio. One might say he's obsessed with them. He fell in love with the radio and the soap operas regularly broadcasted on the device not long after I hired him, which was several years ago. No sooner had I received my medical license and moved into my apartments at 221B Baker Street than I found myself in need of some personal assistance. For one thing, I was too busy being a surgeon to worry about the daily requirements of home ownership, like cooking and cleaning. For another, while I may be fastidious about my own bodily cleanliness, that doesn't mean I want to spend my spare time running around with a dust rag and broom. So I went to an agency, a rude giraffe behind the counter showed me a book with possible cook/housekeepers, and I selected Mr. Javier. We've been happily together ever since.

"That Mr. Bones," Mr. Javier said now, "he is so smart. I think we should keep him, Boss."

"Yes, well, *that's* not going to happen." I ignored the turtle's sad expression as I asked, "So what time will dinner be ready?"

"Not for a while, Boss."

"Great. I have some important things to attend to."

"Soooo," Mr. Javier said, dragging out the word, "how was your day, Boss?"

This was new.

Traditionally, in the years we'd been together, my conversations with the turtle had mostly revolved around the grocery-shopping list and whether or not the place was dusted to my satisfaction. True, he might tell me little bits about his favorite soap opera, but I only listened with half an ear as it was impossible for me to keep Erica and Carly straight. But he'd never asked about my day before. Perhaps because, outside of going off to the Cat Wars, I'd never done anything very interesting in his eyes before today?

So I told him.

I filled him in on the case thus far: how we'd found the dead human in the abandoned house and I'd deduced the cause of death to be cyanide poisoning; how the dog had said the word RACHE scrawled on the wall was not a woman's name interrupted, but rather, the German word for *revenge*; how the dog had concluded that two men had arrived at the abandoned house as friends, driven there by a cab, but only one had remained behind—the dead one, of course; how a woman's gold wedding ring had been found at the scene; how Constable Gibberish had described a tall, funny-smelling man with tiny feet returning to the scene, and the dog assumed he'd come back for the ring.

"So," I said, having completed my tally of

important points, "what do you make of all that?"

"How should I know?" the turtle said. "I have the salmon croquettes to attend to here. I was simply being polite."

I shrugged and went out to the living room where Bones had thoroughly—and disturbingly—made himself at home. He had spread out writing implements and papers all over my table and was hard at work.

Hopping up onto the cushion in front of the bay window, I settled down, curled up on my side and placed a paw over my eyes.

"What are you doing, Catson?" Bones said. "We have telegrams to write! We have a case to solve!"

"Who are the telegrams for?" I asked.

"One is to the *London News*. I want them to put a notice in the early evening edition."

It wasn't even early evening? Without the usual sixteen naps, this day was taking forever.

"What will the notice say?" I asked.

"I'm going to say that we've found a ring, a golden wedding ring."

"HA!" I snorted. "That should bring all the crazies out."

"Perhaps. But hopefully, it'll draw the murderer out too. After all, if he was so eager to retrieve that ring that he was willing to risk getting caught by returning to the scene of the crime … "

It annoyed me to admit it, but the dog had a possible point.

"Then," Bones said, "I'm going to go to the jewelry store and buy an exact copy of the ring to show to whomever answers the notice."

"Sounds marvelous," I muttered, so close to sleep now, I barely knew what I was saying.

"Of course, I'm putting your name down as the finder of the ring."

"Mmmm … What? Why?"

"Because my name is too famous? If the criminal sees 'Sherlock Bones' listed as the finder, he might suspect that something is up and steer clear."

Well, that made sense.

"I'm also saying in the notice," he continued, "that the ring was found in the street. This way, the criminal won't know a connection has been made between the dead body and the ring."

I supposed this made sense too.

"Don't you want to help with the telegrams?" Bones said.

I briefly revived just long enough to consider this. Of course I'd received many telegrams in my day but had never sent one. I was curious. How did it work? But then:

"No, thank you," I said.

"The jewelry store then? Wouldn't you like to go there?"

Perhaps if it was the craft store, I'd be tempted; all that lovely yarn. I tightened my paw more closely around my head. "Only in my dreams … "

As I drifted off, I could have almost sworn I heard Bones say, "Very well. Perhaps I'll send Mr. Javier? He likes getting out now that he has his new jetpack."

CHAPTER NINETEEN

Some time later, we were in the midst of our salmon croquettes when our dinner was interrupted by the sound of the doorbell ringing.

I was going to get up to answer it myself—I certainly wasn't about to let the dog answer *my* door a second time—when I was stopped short by the sight of Mr. Javier, bobbing through with his jetpack.

"Don't worry, Boss!" he cried excitedly as he picked up speed and flew down the stairs. "I've got it! This time, I've finally got it! I've—"

Crash.

I can only imagine how much it hurt his little

turtle head when he smashed into the heavy wooden door.

But whatever the damage, a moment later he was back in the room announcing, "Visitor to see you, Boss, for Mr. Bones too. Says there was a notice in the paper."

I was glad I'd taken my nap so I could be alert right now because this—this!—was exciting.

There was the sound of a slow, heavy tread on the stairs. Apparently, our visitor was not as speedy as a turtle with a jetpack. Well, who is? Bones and I hurried to the living room where we waited eagerly for our visitor to appear.

I don't know what we were expecting, exactly.

Actually, I do know.

We were expecting a man about six feet tall with incredibly tiny feet and a funny smell about him. In short, we were expecting our murderer.

Not a little old lady.

"I'm here about the ring?" her creaky voice stated as she came into view. A scarf covered what little hair she appeared to still have, and her body was so

77

badly stooped over that it was impossible to tell how tall she might be if her form were fully stretched out. Since the upper half of her body was practically parallel to the floor I could not see her eyes as she prompted, "The ring?"

I *knew* Bones's newspaper ad would draw out all the crazies.

Judging from her frayed and torn scarf, she did not appear to be well off. I suspected that, having seen the notice about the ring in the paper, she was likely trying to claim it so that she could immediately sell it for cash.

There was no *way* the golden wedding ring we'd found was hers.

"Of course," Bones said. "I'll go get it for you right away." He turned to exit the room.

Oh, Bones. I groaned inwardly. If I didn't think it would be interpreted as rude, I'd shake my head in disappointment and disgust. The dog was just going to hand over the wedding ring—or at least the copy he'd had made while I was sleeping—to this obvious charlatan? (I always wanted to use the word charlatan, meaning "imposter.") What an idiot. The dog, that is, not the old woman. She was obviously quite clever in her own way.

"There's only one thing," the dog said, pausing in the doorway and then turning to face us once more. "Could you describe it for us, please?"

Could she …

Oh, Bones! I thought. *Good one!* Previously, he had only relaxed her into thinking he would just hand the ring right over, but now he was going to trap her by demanding she provide a description.

"Well," the old woman said after a long pause for deep consideration, "it's gold, isn't it?"

Bones likewise paused for several long moments, then brightly said, "Right! Well, that should do it! I'll just go get … "

I was tempted to slap him. *Well, it's gold, isn't it?* That was enough description to satisfy him that this was the true owner? *Come on, Bones!*

Idiot.

Once more, Bones paused in the doorway, turned. "Yes," he spoke slowly, "the ring is gold, as you say. But can you tell me anything more about it?"

OK, so maybe not *such* an idiot.

"What more can there possibly be?" She looked puzzled. Then: "Unless of course you mean the scratch inside it that looks like the letter Z?"

I shot a questioning glance at Bones, who nodded back at me. I supposed I should have examined the ring more closely earlier, but he apparently had.

"It does indeed have such a marking," he said before finally succeeding in exiting the room.

So, the ring we'd found had the telltale Z on it. Then she really was …

"Then you really are the true owner?" Bones asked, returning with the fake ring, complete with the letter Z, which he promptly handed over.

"Of course not!" She laughed, more of a cackle really.

She *wasn't?* And he just gave her the—

"It's my daughter's!" She laughed that cackle again. "What would one such as I be doing with a ring like this?"

She placed the ring in her skirt pocket and then

slowly turned her back on us.

"How did your daughter lose the ring?" Bones shouted after her.

He must have been thinking of the abandoned building where we'd found it, beneath a murder victim no less. How had it got there?

"Not for me to say, is it?" the woman said. "I'm not the one who lost it."

And then she was gone.

Or at least as quickly as a hunched-over old woman can be gone when first she needs to negotiate a long flight of stairs.

"Well, that's that," I said.

"Of course, *that* is not *that*," Bones said witheringly. Then he raced to the front window. I raced after him and jumped onto the cushion. And so it was that I was able to see what he saw when he pushed the curtains aside:

It was the old woman, below us, hopping into the front passenger side of a cab. For one so old and bent, that hop was disturbingly nimble.

"Mr. Javier!" Bones cried.

Mr. Javier almost instantly hovered in the air beside us. "Yes, Boss?"

How I resented that *Yes, Boss*. Previously, I had been the only Boss around here. But my resentment didn't get much time to fester, not with all the crackling excitement in the air as the dog screamed at the turtle:

"Follow that old woman in that cab!"

CHAPTER TWENTY

"Even you have to admit," the dog said, as we continued to gaze out the window, "it's come in quite handy."

"How's that?"

"Why, the jetpack, of course. Look at Mr. Javier go!"

I watched as Mr. Javier raced through the air, catching up to the horse-drawn cab just as it was about to disappear around the corner.

"I know how to steal a ride on the back of a cab, but even I have been thrown off a time or two. And, as fast as I am," the dog said, "I never could have caught that cab in time, not as quickly as it's moving."

"Yes," I admitted grudgingly, "the jetpack has turned out to have its uses. There's just one problem."

"And what's that?"

"I'm worried about Mr. Javier's head."

"His head?"

I remembered, with a shudder, a few minutes earlier when Mr. Javier had flown down the staircase only to crash into the door once more.

I reminded the dog of this now.

"Huh," he said, mildly disturbed. "I hadn't noticed that part."

For one who had superior powers of observation in so many ways, there really was quite a lot that the dog missed.

"Well, no matter." The dog shrugged, his expression clearing.

"No matter?" I was incensed. "*No matter*? What if Mr. Javier gets brain damage?"

"I hardly think that's going to happen," Bones snorted.

"It will if he keeps banging his head!"

"He has a hard shell."

"On his *back*! *Not* on his *head!*"

The dog waved a dismissive paw. "He'll be fine."

"Fine? Why did you send him to chase after the old woman in the cab anyway?"

The dog yawned, as though the answer to his question was obvious. "Because I want to know where she goes, don't I? Shall we finish our dinner while we wait? There's no telling how long the turtle might be."

So we did that, returning to the dining room and our salmon croquettes.

While we ate, the dog regaled me with stories of his past cases, most involving murders, although there were a few grand thefts and a few examples of "Must Save The Day Before The World As We Know It Ends Completely!" thrown in.

Dinner finished, I rose from the table—*so full*—and made the leisurely stroll into the living room.

"Naptime again?" Bones asked. Wait. Was that a note of sarcasm I detected there?

No big deal. I shrugged, leapt up onto the cushion, curled up, and closed my eyes.

"You're finally catching on," I said. "What about you? Don't you need to nap? After all, as you pointed out, who knows how long it'll take Mr. Javier to return?"

"Yes, our turtle may be a while yet."

Our—

"But there'll be no napping for me," Bones said, before I could object. Really, *our* turtle? "When there's a case going on, I never sleep until it's solved."

I might have known.

CHAPTER TWENTY-ONE

"It must have been a disguise!"

I woke to the sound of the dog being his usual excitable self. He was speaking in exclamations and running around in circles on the carpet. *Give him another moment*, I thought, *and he'll start chasing his own tail.*

"What's going on?" I asked, groggy.

"Wake up, Catson," the dog ordered. "The turtle is back!"

Now I was fully awake, and sure enough, there was Mr. Javier.

"Mr. Javier was just telling me the most

extraordinary thing," the dog said, before Mr. Javier could even open his mouth to speak, "that when the cab reached its destination, a man stepped out of it, *not* an old woman."

"It's true, Boss," Mr. Javier said eagerly.

It took me a moment to register that when Mr. Javier said this, he was looking at Bones. There it was again: the turtle calling the dog "Boss."

Before I could object to this—or better yet, correct him—the turtle continued.

"As the man walked away, I peered inside the cab. You know, I figured, maybe the man had already been inside when the old woman first got in? Maybe she was still in there?"

"And?" I prompted.

"And there was no one else inside, not even a cabdriver, Boss." At least now he was calling the right person "Boss."

"How is that possible?" I demanded.

"As I said, it must have been a disguise!" the dog said.

"Why do you think that?" I asked.

"Elementary," the dog said, although initially, I failed to see how this could be so. "There never *was* an old woman to start with. It was someone else, wearing an old-woman disguise."

"This is just like the story of Snow White!" Now I was the eager one.

"Excuse me?" the dog said.

"Snow White! You know, when she's staying with the dwarves, and there's a knock at the door, and at first it seems to be a kindly old woman, all hunched over, a head covering obscuring most of her hair, but in reality it's the evil queen, and then she gives Snow White the poisoned apple?"

"This is nothing like that." The dog snorted. Then he turned his attention to Mr. Javier. "How tall was the man who stepped out of the cab?"

Mr. Javier jetted up to approximately six feet off the ground. "About this tall, Boss."

Six feet tall?

"Oh," Mr. Javier added, "and he had really tiny feet."

Six feet tall, with really tiny feet?

Earlier in the evening, I'd thought we were being silly, expecting the murderer to just walk through the door.

Yet, that is precisely what had happened. The murderer *had* waltzed right in and had not only tried, but *succeeded*, in claiming the ring. And then we had returned to our salmon croquettes.

What a bold chap this murderer was!

Then it hit me:

Just a short time ago, I had been face to face with a murderer, one who had stood as close to me as Mr. Javier was floating now.

CHAPTER TWENTY-TWO

It's a chilling thought, imagining one's self standing in such close proximity to such a terrible person. But I didn't have long to think about it, because now the dog was pestering the turtle for more information:

"Where did the tall man go after the cab left him off?"

"I'm sorry, Boss." The turtle looked embarrassed. Well, as embarrassed as a turtle *can* look. "I was so astonished by there being no old woman in the cab that by the time I got over the shock, the man had disappeared."

"That's quite all right, Mr. Javier," the dog surprisingly soothed. "You've performed well tonight, and the salmon croquettes were marvelous."

That last part was certainly true.

"So what do we do now?" I asked.

Before anyone could answer, however, the doorbell rang again.

"I'll get it, Bosses, I'll get it!" Mr. Javier cried, jetting off.

Could it be our murderer? I wondered as we waited for the turtle to return. But why would the murderer come back here? Unless it was to shut us up? I thought about what a murderer shutting us up might entail. Then I thought about hiding under the sofa. When it comes to a choice between fight or flight, I almost always go for flight. But then I straightened my spine. Now was no time for hiding in fear under a piece of comfy furniture. I had, after all, served in the Cat Wars.

But when Mr. Javier returned, the person accompanying him was neither an old woman nor was it a tall man with tiny feet.

It was Inspector No One Very Important and he had an important announcement to make:

"I've arrested a suspect."

Well, blow me down again.

CHAPTER TWENTY-THREE

"You've arrested a *suspect*?" Bones was as bowled over by this news as I was. "*You've* arrested a suspect?"

I could understand the dog's shock. Who would have ever guessed that Inspector No One Very Important would be allowed to arrest someone, much less solve the case?

It seemed to me that in addition to being surprised by this news, the dog was also a bit anxious and grumpy about it. Perhaps he didn't like the idea of the public detectives solving a case before he did?

"We managed to locate the boardinghouse where,

er, John Smith and his secretary were staying just prior to, er, John Smith's murder," said Inspector No One Very Important.

"John Smith?" I puzzled. "Er, John Smith? Now, why does that name ring a bell … "

"Remember?" Bones prompted impatiently. "The dead body? When we found him in the abandoned building, you requested that we all call him by John Smith rather than use his real name?"

"Right, right." With so few opportunities for proper naps, my mind was getting a bit muddled on the details.

"Please, Inspector, er—" I paused, realizing that I couldn't call him Inspector No One Very Important to his face. "Do go on."

"As I was saying, we managed to locate the boardinghouse where, er, John Smith and his secretary were staying."

"My," I said, impressed, "you really *have* been busy!"

It never even occurred to me that while Bones and I were conducting our own investigation, the public detectives might actually be getting anything done.

Wait a second. Did I just say *our*?

"The boardinghouse," Inspector No One Very Important continued, "is owned by—"

He went ahead and named yet another one of those more involved human names. I think it was French because it began with "Madame."

"Wait, wait, wait!" I held up a paw to stop him. "This simply won't do!"

"How's that?"

"Wouldn't it be simpler," I said, suggesting the obvious, "if we just referred to this woman who owns the boardinghouse as Fifi?"

Inspector No One Very Important and Bones both looked at me with what looked suspiciously like shock. Then Bones shrugged.

"I don't think it makes much difference." Bones turned to Inspector No One Very Important. "Do you?"

"No." Inspector No One Very Important shrugged back. "I reckon not." Then, clearing his throat, he continued. "We learned from Fifi that, er, John Smith, was quite the troublesome guest."

"How so?" Bones asked.

"Was he one of those incredibly obnoxious types?" I asked, casting a meaningful look upon Bones. "You know the type—shows up uninvited and then just stays and stays until you think you'll go mad?"

"Not at all," Inspector No One Very Important said. "He was out of control one night and tried to kiss Fifi's daughter."

"And *that's* why he was killed!" I said. "In order to get back at him for trying to kiss her daughter, the boardinghouse woman murdered him!"

CHAPTER
TWENTY-FOUR

"Of course not!" Inspector No One Very Important said. "*That's* not what happened!"

"It isn't?"

"No! Fifi simply kicked him out."

"Oh," I said, disappointed that his answer wasn't what I had expected. "Well, I suppose that's not terribly surprising, is it? If he tried to kiss my daughter, I'd kick him out too. Not that I've ever had a daughter. Or a son for that matter. Or a litter."

"Catson?" Bones said.

"Yes, Bones?"

"Do you think we might let the inspector get on

with his tale?"

Oh. Right.

"Yes, well," Inspector No One Very Important continued. "After, er, John Smith was evicted, he didn't exactly stay evicted."

"He *didn't*?" I said. I hadn't seen *that* coming.

"No," Inspector No One Very Important said. "According to Fifi, he returned to the boardinghouse later the same night and tried to kiss Fifi's daughter *again*."

"No!" I was horrified on Fifi's daughter's behalf.

"*Yes*," Inspector No One Very Important reassured me.

"The scoundrel," I said.

"Indeed."

"So then what happened?"

"Well, he was attacked, of course."

"By the daughter?" I said, eager once more. "So it wasn't Fifi who murdered him. It was her daughter?"

"Of course not!"

"Oh." I was puzzled. I'd been sure I had it that time. "Who, then? Who attacked, er, John Smith?"

"It was *the brother*!" Inspector No One Very Important said, eyes flashing.

"Wait, wait, wait! Hold on here!" I held one front paw straight in the air. "Time out!"

"What appears to be the problem?" Inspector No One Very Important asked.

"The brother? *The brother*?" I turned to the dog. "Bones, help me out here. Am I missing something? I'm quite certain a *brother* wasn't part of the story before."

"If there's a Fifi and she's got a daughter," the dog said, "I see no logical reason why the daughter can't have a brother."

"Oh, pah." I waved at him disgustedly. "You're no help."

"Perhaps you'd like to tell us," Bones addressed Inspector No One Very Important, "what exactly the brother did?"

"Well, he chased, er, John Smith out of the house, didn't he?" Inspector No One Very Important spoke as if this must be obvious when, really, nothing seemed obvious to me anymore. "By his own admission, the brother chased John Smith down the street and when he caught him, he beat him a bit about the head."

"And *that's* how he murdered him?" I said. "But er, John Smith was killed with poison."

"He was," Inspector No One Very Important agreed. "At any rate, the brother claims it wasn't him that murdered, er, John Smith. Claims, er, John Smith was still alive when last he saw him. That somehow John Smith escaped his clutches and got away."

"So then the brother *isn't* the murderer?"

"Who knows? Of course, we arrested him anyway."

"*That's* who you arrested?"

"Why not?"

"Because hitting a man who tried to kiss your sister does not constitute murder? Because you don't have any real evidence? Because you might have the wrong man?"

"Well, who's to say that he *didn't* commit the murder? And anyway, we have to arrest someone, don't we?"

CHAPTER TWENTY-FIVE

My mind reeled. Frankly, it wasn't how I thought our justice system worked.

At last, I simply threw up my paws. If they had made an arrest, I might as well have a snack.

"Anyone hungry?" I offered.

Inspector No One Very Important scrunched up his face in what apparently passed for deep thought for him. "I could eat," he decided.

"Bones?" I prompted.

"Always," the dog said.

"Mr. Javier!" I called. "Are you still awake?"

Mr. Javier entered the room slowly, in his usual

four-legged fashion but with the jetpack still attached to his back. Perhaps he'd decided to try being a little more cautious with his device, at least indoors. After all, there was the threat of all that crashing, particularly into walls.

"Of course I'm awake, Boss," Mr. Javier said. "I try my best to be awake whenever you're awake and might need me, which, I must confess, can be a bit challenging."

"Challenging?" Was I a demanding boss and had never realized it before?

"Wake, sleep, wake, sleep, wake, sleep—about sixteen times on the average day. Except for today. Today it's been almost all awake."

"Yes, well, I'm sorry for any inconvenience. You have the dog to blame for that. But since you're up anyway, do you think you might prepare us all a snack? What do we have in the kitchen?"

"A little bit of this, probably too much of that. But really, Boss, we're no longer limited to what's already in the kitchen."

"We're not?"

"Of course not! We can get the takeout!"

"The takeout?"

"Yes, the takeout, Boss! The takeout, the takeout, the takeout!"

My, the turtle was working himself into a tizzy.

"You know, Boss," Mr. Javier prompted, "the takeout? You get those menus they shove under the door, then you call the dining establishment, and you tell them exactly what you want. Then, they tell you how much it will be and that you can pick it up in ten to twenty minutes, and you go out to pick it up. Within a half hour, you have a wonderful meal in the privacy of your own home that no one under your roof actually had to prepare!"

Clearly, he had given this a lot of thought.

"We could never get the takeout before," Mr. Javier said, "because by the time I would get it home, it would be the next day or even the day after that. The food might be stale or maybe your desire for it would have passed. But now? With my jetpack? We can get takeout from *anywhere*! What's your pleasure, Boss? We could get the Chinese, Japanese,

Thai, Vietnamese, Italian, Chicago deep-dish pizza, New York thin-crust pizza, New Haven white clam pizza, Australian shrimp on the barbie, Lebanese, Ecuadorian—"

"Mr. Javier." I held up a paw to stop him before the turtle reeled off every ethnic cuisine on the planet. Was there a continent he'd missed? I didn't think we had time to wait and see what he came up with for Antarctica.

"Yes, Boss?"

"You decide," I said magnanimously.

"*Oh*." The turtle's eyes went wide. Well, as wide as a turtle's eyes can get. "*Oh!*"

Within moments, the turtle had jetted over to the telephone, a black contraption that sits on an occasional table I hardly ever use. It's the phone I hardly use since I don't care much for talking on it; the table I do use occasionally. Mr. Javier removed the receiver from the base of the telephone, dialed a number, spoke rapidly and replaced the receiver. Then he flew down the stairs without thought for his own safety—*crash*—and out the door.

It truly was amazing.

Within a half hour, the turtle was back with dozens of little white cartons. While he was gone, we had rehashed the case so far. All the things I'd told Mr. Javier about while he was preparing the salmon croquettes were included, with the addition of the parts about: the old lady coming to retrieve the ring in answer to the newspaper notice; Mr. Javier following the cab and seeing *not* an old lady exit, but rather a tall man matching the description of our murderer; finally arriving at the information about Smith's stay at the boardinghouse, Smith's kissing of the daughter, Smith's beating by the brother, and the ridiculous—to my mind—arrest the public detectives had made as a result. In the remaining time, Bones had showed Inspector No One Very Important some fencing moves while I mostly yawned.

"What did you get, Mr. Javier?" I asked as he began to set the meal out on the dining room table.

"I thought, Boss, for this first takeout experience, we would go traditional, so I got Chinese. Next time, we can branch out a bit, be more adventurous. I got the wonton soup, the spareribs, the egg rolls, the Moo Shu pork, the shrimp with cashews, the—"

He reeled off so many dishes, I feared what effect Mr. Javier's new obsession might have on my wallet, let alone my waistline. But it all smelled so good, I could hardly complain.

Just as we sat down for our snack and *just* as I was reaching with my chopsticks for a plump jumbo shrimp, the doorbell rang.

"I got it, Boss!" Mr. Javier cried. "I got it!"

A moment, one crash, and some heavy footsteps clomping up the stairs later, Inspector Strange walked into the dining room.

"I'm afraid," he said, "there's been another murder."

CHAPTER TWENTY-SIX

"*A*nother murder?" Dumbfounded, I dropped my shrimp. "But we never properly solved the *first* murder!"

"Well," Inspector No One Very Important put in, "we did arrest the brother."

"*Oh.*" I waved a disgustedly dismissive paw at him. "Obviously, *he* didn't do it."

"Catson does have a point," Bones said. "Although, while I usually deal in murders one at a time, I don't suppose I mind taking them in bunches. So, who's the new dead body?"

"I already filled them in on what we learned at the

boardinghouse," Inspector No One Very Important informed Inspector Strange.

"Fine, fine," Inspector Strange said irritably. Who could blame him? Inspector No One Very Important seemed to have that effect upon people.

"Oh," Inspector No One Very Important added, "by the way, we've all agreed to refer to the woman who runs the boardinghouse as Fifi."

"Fine, fine," Inspector Strange said again.

"The new dead body?" Bones prompted with an admirable degree of patience. "You were about to tell us about the new dead body?"

"Yes, and I would have right away if I hadn't been sidetracked by—never mind. I was about to say that I tracked down the secretary of, er, John Smith."

"Does the secretary have a name?" I asked.

"Of course he has a name!" Inspector Strange said. "Or I suppose I should say he *had* a name."

Had—that sounded ominous, at least for the secretary.

"Do you think," I suggested helpfully, "that we might simply refer to him as the secretary?"

"That's exactly what I *was* doing!"

Grouchy, grouchy.

"And where did you track the secretary down?" Bones asked.

"In another boardinghouse," Inspector Strange said. "Unfortunately, though, my timing was a bit off."

"Off?" I asked. "How so?"

"Well, he was already dead, wasn't he?" Inspector Strange snorted. "It would have been more convenient of him to wait until after I had a chance to speak with him before he went and got himself murdered."

"Yes, I'm sure *his* murder was very inconvenient for *you*," I said dryly.

Inspector Strange shot me a look.

What? I think I know when a little sarcasm is called for, which is almost always.

"When I arrived at the boardinghouse," Inspector Strange said, "the owner told me that the secretary had said he was expecting a visitor. The owner assumed I was that visitor and I didn't correct him.

But when I got to the secretary's door and knocked, there was no answer; when I tried the doorknob, it was locked from the inside. And, yet, the owner swore he hadn't seen the secretary leave."

"The plot thickens," Bones said.

"Yes," Inspector Strange said. "It has a bad habit of doing that, doesn't it?"

"So what did you do?" I asked.

"I broke the door down, of course," Inspector Strange said, clearly proud of his strength. "That's when I saw the dead body, this one somehow killed in a locked room."

Locked room? I'd encountered mysteries in my lives before, but I never thought I'd encounter one involving a locked room!

"But how did the murderer get in or out," I asked, "if the door was locked from the inside?"

"Elementary, my dear Catson," Bones said.

"It *is*?"

"Of course." Bones regarded Inspector Strange. "After gaining entry to the room and finding the body, you noticed that a window was open. And

111

looking out the window, you found evidence that a ladder had been used to reach it. Perhaps the ladder was even still in position there?"

Inspector Strange, Inspector No One Very Important, and I all stared at the dog in wonder.

"And how did you know *that*?" Inspector Strange demanded.

"Elementary," Bones said again. "A dead body found on the second story; a door locked from within—what other explanation could there be?"

Huh.

"The murderer had to get in somehow," Bones said. "After all, this isn't some fairy story with magic and little elves, is it? If not by the door, then there must be a window. If the window is on the second story, there must be a ladder to get to the window; for, however tall our murderer might be, he can't be *that* tall, not two stories' worth."

Huh again.

Inspector Strange shook his head in wonder, before continuing. "I leaned out the window and saw a boy down below, on the ground. I asked him if he'd seen a man on the ladder earlier. He said that, yes, that he'd seen a tall man with really tiny feet using it and had assumed him to be a worker. Seeing my expression, the boy said he hoped he hadn't done anything wrong. I told him that, of course he hadn't, not unless he included letting a murderer get away with murder."

How sensitive.

"Next," Inspector Strange said, "I investigated the body."

"How had he been killed?" Bones asked. "Not another poisoning, I expect."

"How did you know that this one hadn't been poisoned too, Bones?" Inspector Strange asked.

"I'm educated." The dog shrugged. "And I made a guess."

"A good one at that." Inspector Strange nodded firmly. "I found the body by the window. Unlike the body of, er, John Smith in the abandoned building, this one had been stabbed."

Oh my. I'm not usually given to queasiness at the thought of death. I'd been through the Cat Wars after all. As a doctor there, I'd seen a lot. But stabbed? It was a bit much.

"Oh, and one other thing," Inspector Strange said.

"Yes?" Bones asked.

"Much as it kills me to say it, you were right."

"Obviously." The dog snorted. "But about what exactly?"

"The motive," Inspector Strange said, "it was revenge."

CHAPTER TWENTY-SEVEN

"How do you know that?" I asked.

"Let me guess," the dog said, not bothering to wait for Inspector Strange's response. "Over the secretary's body was written the German word for 'revenge,' RACHE. Despite what I'd told you when we'd seen that written over the first body, you continued to believe that it was an incomplete writing of a woman's name. But when you saw it a second time, even you couldn't convince yourself that the writer had once again been interrupted at precisely the same moment. And so, despite your reluctance to admit it, you were forced to see that I was right all along." He paused. "Am I right?"

"Sad to say," Inspector Strange said, "that pretty much sums it up."

"Oh, the poor secretary," I said.

"Why the poor secretary?" Inspector Strange asked.

"It's the way he died," I said. "I should think it would be bad enough, spending your life working in service to another being." I paused, looking at Mr. Javier and thinking about what I'd just said. I shook the thought off—it was one for another time. "But then, on top of that, to be murdered just like your employer, as though paying for what *he* did—"

"Oh," Inspector Strange cut me off, "I'd say the secretary had enough of his own sins to pay for."

"And what does *that* mean?" I demanded.

Instead of answering, Inspector Strange sniffed the air. "Do I smell Chinese food?"

"Yes," I said. "We were just sitting down to eat when you came to call."

"I am a bit hungry," he hinted.

Having had my meal interrupted by news of a

second murder, I realized I was still hungry myself.

"Would you like some?" I offered, leading the way toward the dining area. "We have wonton soup, spareribs, egg rolls, shrimp with—"

But as I saw when we stepped over the threshold into the dining room, we didn't have any of those things anymore. All we had were a pile of empty takeout containers and one very full-looking public detective.

"Inspector!" I said, appalled. "You ate all the food? *Yourself?*"

"I'm sorry," Inspector No One Very Important said with a burp, looking ashamed at his own behavior. "I couldn't help myself."

"Oh, Inspector." I shook my head. Now what were we going to do? "Mr. Javier!" I bellowed.

"Yes, Boss?"

I jumped back a step. The way he could now just suddenly appear in a room did take some getting used to.

"I'll need you to get us some more food," I said, "since *some* of us can't seem to control ourselves."

"The takeout, Boss?" Mr. Javier was eager. "Can we do the takeout again, please?"

"Yes, fine, whatever you want," I said brusquely. "Just not Chinese again. That didn't work out so well the first time."

"Right away, Boss."

And he was gone.

To his credit, the crash was a little quieter this time.

"Now where were we?" I asked as we four took seats at the dining room table, still covered with empty takeout containers.

"Inspector Strange was about to explain to us what he meant when he said the secretary had his own sins to pay for," the dog provided.

"Yes," Inspector Strange said. "Funny thing. Outside of the dead body and the message on the wall, there was hardly anything else in the room. In fact, the only things the secretary had on him were a book and a pipe—smoking is a filthy habit—and a box with pills in it."

"*Pills?*" Bones said.

"Huh," Inspector Strange said. "I'd have guessed

you would be more curious about the book."

"Why would I be curious about the book?"

"Because it might be an important clue? Don't you even want to know the title?"

The dog snorted. "The only thing the presence of the book indicates is that the secretary hated waiting in line, and always brought a book with him whenever he went anywhere in order to keep his mind occupied. Which is exactly what I do. It's a habit I highly recommend. Of course, now that I have Mr. Javier, I shouldn't think I'd need to worry about doing my own shopping anymore."

"You don't *have* Mr. Ja—" I began to object.

But the dog cut me off. "No, the book doesn't signify anything more than that the secretary had an active mind. Of the three items mentioned, the only one that *does* potentially signify anything are those pills. Now, what did you do with them? Bring them to the lab? Have them analyzed?"

"No." Inspector Strange produced a pillbox. "I have them right here."

"You have them right ... Are you *insane*?"

"Why is it that, at least once every case, you ask me that question?"

"Because I suspect it might be true?" The dog shook his head. "I can't believe you are just strolling around the city with what is undoubtedly the best clue we've uncovered yet."

"*We've*—" Inspector Strange began to object.

But the dog cut him off with a snap of the paw. "Hand that over, please."

Inspector Strange obeyed.

Bones opened the lid on the pillbox, studied the contents inside.

"Unless I'm wrong," he said, "and that's highly unlikely, one or more of these pills contain poison."

"How can you be sure?" I asked.

"That's the thing," the dog said. "Without further testing, it's impossible to know for certain."

He shifted his attention from the pillbox to everyone sitting around him at the table, considering each of us in turn.

"So," he said finally with a grin so wide he could have swallowed a small cat, "who wants to volunteer?"

CHAPTER TWENTY-EIGHT

The three of us stared at the dog, our mouths hanging open.

I was the first to recover.

"You want to use one of us ... as a guinea pig? You want one of us ... to volunteer to take poison? You can't be serious!"

"Of course not, my dear Catson," the dog said. And there was that wide grin again. "Well, maybe just a bit."

"Do you think those might be what killed er, John Smith?" I said. "If so, I can simply sniff them for you. If they smell of almonds, there's our answer."

"Ah, but what if they smell of almonds and yet they're *not* laced with cyanide?" he said. "What if they're simply some harmless almond-scented pills? No, I'm afraid we need more conclusive evidence here than your nose can provide."

Before I could respond, the dog rose from his seat at the table, pocketing the pillbox in the palm of his paw.

"Where are you going with those pills?" I said as he began to move away from the table.

"Well," he said, as though the answer must be obvious, "if I can't get any volunteers here, I shall have to look elsewhere, won't I?"

"Where are you going?" I called, more desperately. But he was soon through the doorway and out of view, his voice traveling back to us:

"I need to see a dog about a man."

CHAPTER TWENTY-NINE

While the inspectors shouted their outrage (Strange: "How dare he take off without consulting us!") and grumbled their displeasure (No One Very Important: "It's our case too, you know"), I spent several minutes considering whether to take a nap.

I was so tired, but I wasn't accustomed to napping with a human in the house, never mind two humans. What if, while I was sleeping, they tried to pet me? Or, worse, pick me up and place me in their laps?

I shuddered at the thought.

Tired, hungry. Hungry, tired. I'd never been so

much of either in my life, let alone both at the same time, not even during the Cat Wars.

I considered excusing myself and disappearing into one of the bedrooms, which I almost never use, the cushion in front of the bay window being so much nicer for napping. Surely, behind closed doors, I could rest for a bit, safe from the threat of being petted or picked up? And, you know, maybe I'd find a little something to snack on back there?

I was about to do just that, when a lot of activity happened all at once.

First, Mr. Javier came back with his beloved takeout.

"I got Lebanese, Boss!" the turtle announced. "This time, I got Lebanese!"

He began excitedly taking containers out of his big bag.

"I got the baba ghanouj," he said, "and the kibbeh, and the hummus, and the tabbouleh, and for you, the shish taouk, which are like grilled chicken skewers—"

Except for the part about the chicken, I had no

idea what he was talking about. It was all Lebanese to me. But it all smelled so heavenly, and I was so hungry, I didn't care what I was eating.

I was just reaching for a carton when the doorbell rang.

"Should I get that, Boss?" Mr. Javier asked, looking torn. I could well understand why he should feel that way. After all, he must be hungry too.

"Just keep dishing up the food, Mr. Javier." I waved a fork at him. "I can't imagine who that could be at this hour. And look around you: Anyone who should be inside is already right here."

Then it hit me:

The dog still wasn't back.

And then it came to me, the last thing the dog had said before he headed out the door was: "I need to see a dog about a man."

What had he meant? Where had he gone and where was he now?

"If no one else is going to get that, I suppose I'll have to," the dog called from somewhere in the house.

Wait a second. When had the dog returned? And why was the dog roaming freely around the rest of my house?

Before I could yell or object, he bounded through the room and down the stairs to open the door, returning accompanied by …

"*Puppies?*" I cried. "What are all these *puppies* doing in *my* house?"

CHAPTER THIRTY

I rubbed at my eyes.

But no matter how hard I rubbed, every time I opened my eyes, the puppies were still there.

I counted: one, two, three, four, five, six. If I had to take a guess, I'd say they were Cocker Spaniels. They looked ridiculous, all so small, as they bounded around Bones.

I wanted to believe this was just a hallucination brought on by lack of food or sleep.

Puppies? In *my* house?

"I did tell you," Bones said with a wry smile, "that I had to see a dog about a man."

"A dog, fine," I said. "One dog." Then I pointed at the sestet. "But that's not one, it's six. And it's not a dog, it's *puppies*."

And, those puppies were having a field day, scampering all over my home, snuffling their snouts through all of my possessions.

"I suppose you're right, my dear Catson. But if I'd said 'I need to see six puppies about a man,' it wouldn't have really had the same ring to it, would it?"

"Just a second, Bones," I said, holding up a paw to stop him from doing anything rash. Even if I didn't like the idea of having puppies in my home, I didn't want to see them murdered right in front of me either. Which is exactly what Bones was about to do. He would administer the various tablets from the pillbox to the various little puppies and then watch to see if any—all?—fell down dead.

"Just a second *what?*" Bones asked with some irritation.

"Just a second for me to cover my eyes," I said, squeezing them shut. Almost instantly, though, I snapped them back open again. I couldn't believe how cowardly I was being. Was I just going to stand there, eyes squeezed shut, while Bones killed relatively innocent puppies in the name of scientific research? I had been to the Cat Wars. I was made of sterner stuff than this.

"I won't let you hurt them!" I said, throwing my body between the dog and the puppies, spreading my arms wide to protectively shield them behind me. I couldn't believe I was about to try to save puppies, but there you have it.

"What *are* you talking about, my dear Catson?" Bones demanded, more irritable still.

"Yes, what is she talking about?" Inspector Strange asked Bones.

Oh. The humans. For a moment, I'd forgotten they were there. Particularly Inspector No One Very Important, as he didn't really say very much. Although he ate plenty.

"You know," Inspector Strange added, "her reactions to things are often so strange, I sometimes have trouble remembering, let alone believing, that she's a real doctor."

Oh! Who was he to be calling anyone else strange?

"You were about to kill them!" I cried, raising a paw in accusation and pointing it straight at the dog's face. "You were going to give the puppies those pills so you could see which ones wound up dead! I simply won't have it in my house!"

Bones burst out laughing. "Don't be absurd!"

"I fail to see how—"

"I wasn't going to harm the puppies." The dog continued to chuckle, completely unable to contain his mirth. "I wasn't going to *kill* them!"

"You weren't?" I dropped my paws. "What then?"

"I was merely going to introduce you to my young associates," he said.

"*Them*? They're your"—I could barely bring myself to choke out the words—"young associates?"

"Of course." He turned to the puppies. "Boys, may I introduce to you Dr. Jane Catson."

And he proceeded to go through what by now had become his usual dog-and-pony show, trotted out whenever introducing me to someone new. You know: "This is my partner"; "Yes, the cat's a doctor";

"Yes, the doctor's a girl"; and "blah, blah, blah."
Apparently, in this scenario, I was the pony.

CHAPTER THIRTY-ONE

"Stop, Bones. I know who *I* am," I said, irritable now. "But who are *they*? And what are *they* doing in *my* house?"

"Why, they're the Baker Street Regulars, aren't they?" he said, as though the answer must be obvious. How thoroughly annoying. Not to mention, that the street he'd named happened to be the very same one in my address, and yet I'd never heard of these puppies before now.

"The Baker Street *who*?" I demanded.

"Well, they used to be known as the Cambridge Street Regulars," he said, naming the street upon which resided Our Mutual Friend, the one who had essentially started this whole mess in the first place. "But," Bones continued, "it doesn't make much sense, does it, for me to keep referring to them like that when I live here now."

"You do *not* now—"

"I sometimes use the Baker Street Regulars to help out with my cases. They're all strays, every last one. It's good for them to have something useful to do. Keeps them off the streets. Of course, technically, being strays, they're always on the streets. Well, except for right now."

"I'm sure they must be quite helpful," I said, already feeling a headache building.

"Oh, we are, sir!" one of the young pups piped up. But then he looked embarrassed as he corrected, "I mean, ma'am."

"This cheeky young pup," said Bones proudly, "is Waggins. You might say he's the leader of the pack."

"Pleased to meet you, I'm sure," I said dryly.

I noticed that while Bones had introduced me to his young associates, he hadn't bothered to introduce them to the humans. It was nice to think I was getting special treatment. But I couldn't let such rudeness stand.

"Don't you think," I said to Bones, "that it would only be polite for you to introduce your little friends to Inspector Strange and Inspector, er, too?"

"No need," Inspector Strange said. "We've all met before, many times."

I went straight from feeling special to feeling like an outsider in my own home. Well, at the very least, I could still be a good host. Plus, my stomach was growling.

"In that case," I said, "since we're all friends here now, or something approximating it, perhaps we should share a meal together. Mr. Javier jetted out for Lebanese and while I haven't had the chance to taste any of it yet, I can assure you it all looks most delicious—"

"'Fraid there's no time for that, ma'am," Waggins said.

"There's not?" I raised the whiskers above my eyes at him. "Not even some hummus?"

"No, ma'am." He turned to Bones. "I summoned that cab you wanted and it's been waiting right outside."

"Cab?" I demanded. "When did you call for a cab?"

"Waggins!" Bones cried. "Why didn't you say something earlier? By all means, send the cabbie up!"

As the puppy scampered away and down the stairs, I asked the dog, "Send the cabbie up? Isn't it the usual practice, when a cab arrives, to go down and get into the cab and go away? If I'm not mistaken, I do believe you have things backward here."

While I was saying this, the tiny part of my brain that was as yet not shot from sheer exhaustion wondered: *Perhaps Bones was finally going away ... for good?*

"Not at all," the dog answered me. "I need the cabbie to come up to help me with this." He pointed to a large steamer trunk, the kind that might be used when going on a long ocean voyage or rail journey. Where had that come from? It certainly wasn't mine.

"As extraordinary as I am," Bones continued, "even I cannot move something of that size without help. And it is, after all, one of a cabbie's duties to help a customer load his luggage."

"Where are you going?" I asked.

Perhaps he had found somewhere else to stay while he sought more permanent lodgings? Good! So why, then, did I not feel entirely happy? It must be because I was so tired.

"All in good time," Bones said. "All in good time."

It was such a mysterious thing to say. We cats are mysterious. But dogs? Everything about them is right on the surface. What you see is what you get. Well, except for this one apparently. How annoying.

While we waited for the puppy to return with the cabbie—the other puppies running in circles as puppies will do; the inspectors looking confused at the turn of events and then annoyed at their own confusion; the turtle bobbing up near the ceiling— Bones opened his trunk and brought out a shiny object that looked like two silver bracelets attached at the center by a chain. He offered them to Inspector Strange.

"What are those?" Inspector Strange asked with a derisive sniff. "I don't want to be your *girl*friend!"

Why is it that anything associated with "girl" is always deemed some sort of insult? You always hear humans say things like, "You run like a girl!" or "He screamed like a little girl!" How is that an insult? After all, *I'm* a girl. I'm a girl and a doctor and I can run as fast as anyone. Well, I could before I was injured in the Cat Wars.

"Nor do I want you to be," answered Bones, "and please don't refer to girls in such a disdainful fashion. It is so backward-thinking of you."

Did my ears deceive me? Did Bones just say that? For the briefest of seconds there, I could have kissed him. *Yuck.* As if I would ever! I wiped the back of one paw against my mouth as though wiping away the phantom kiss and its resulting dog germs. Perish the thought.

"No," Bones went on. "These are handcuffs. Do you not know what handcuffs are? They are something I invented and am in the process of perfecting. They are most useful when apprehending criminals. I thought you might have some use for them. After all, I think it's a bit much for you to expect criminals to just come along with you quietly once you've apprehended them."

Those things he held in his paws, they did look handy; cuffy too. Still …

"You invented those?" I said.

"Of course," he said, "just like I invented the jetpack for Mr. Javier. Did I not tell you that in addition to being the world's greatest detective I am also an inventor?"

"You did not," I said, still skeptical. "What else have you invented then?"

The dog cast a meaningful look upward at the lighting fixture hanging over our very heads.

"Oh, come on!" I said. "You expect me to believe that Thomas Alva Edison stole the idea for the light bulb from you and not James Swan?"

The dog closed his eyes as he nodded in a gesture that could have been humble but somehow wasn't.

"You've seen my handiwork with what the jetpack can do, have you not?" he said.

"Yes, but that's a far cry from—"

"I have no use for your silly bracelets!" Inspector Strange scoffed, interrupting.

"Very well then." Bones set the handcuffs down to one side of the steamer trunk. "We'll just leave them there for now."

No sooner had he finished speaking than there came the sound of the door opening, followed by the scamper of Waggins returning, a much heavier tread trailing his eager puppy feet.

Bones turned to me then, his eyes flashing excitement.

"Now," he said, "the real fun begins."

CHAPTER THIRTY-THREE

What was he *talking* about?

I did not get the chance to pose my question aloud, however, for now Waggins was back among us and, with him, the cabbie.

He was a tall human, this cabbie. Were my ceilings of the low sort you sometimes hear about, more typically found in older pubs, his head would no doubt scrape against it.

"The pup said you needed help with a trunk?" the cabbie said in what can only be described as a surly fashion. I must say, the help these days. It's not like when I hired Mr. Javier, that's for certain.

"Yes, my good chap!" Bones said, all friendly good cheer and politeness himself, as though taking no notice whatsoever of the cabbie's surly rudeness. "It's this trunk right here." He indicated. "If you could be so good as to … "

The cabbie bent to the task and—

CHAPTER THIRTY-FOUR

Bones, in a move swifter than I would have thought him capable, reached down beside the trunk, snatched up the handcuffs, slapped them around the cabbie's wrists—they did make a satisfying *click!*—and announced, to the surprise of all assembled:

"Mr. Jefferson Hope, I hereby arrest you for the murders of, er, John Smith and the secretary!"

CHAPTER THIRTY-FIVE

*Wh*at just happened here???

CHAPTER THIRTY-SIX

No, really. What just happened?

I had no time to ask because, all at once, his hands cuffed behind his back, Mr. Jefferson Hope—if that really was his name and not just something the dog had dreamed up—made for my bay window, hurling his body against it with such force that the lower window broke, raining glass down upon my precious cushion.

As the tall man moved, so moved the public detectives, grabbing onto his restrained arms and tackling him to the floor before he could make his escape. The most horrible melee ensued with furniture crashing and limbs flying. For a restrained man, and even with two humans against his one, he was still capable of putting up quite a fight.

"Do you think we should help?" I asked, raising my voice to be heard over all the loud thumping and crashing. "I'm not particularly keen on fighting," I added.

"I am." The dog smiled. "But let them handle it." He indicated the inspectors with twin juts of his chin. "It is the one thing they're good at."

Meanwhile, no doubt excited by the excess of noise, the puppies, with the exception of Waggins, were scampering all over the place, getting into every nook and cranny of my home, as puppies will do.

"Waggins!" Bones called over the thuds. "In future, perhaps it would be best if you left the puppies outside and simply came up yourself?"

"Future?" I cried, *not* like a girl. "There isn't going to be any *future*!"

But the dog didn't answer me, only smiling as the public detectives finally wrestled "Mr. Jefferson Hope" to his feet.

"And anyway," I said, quite irritable now, "how do you know that's the murderer? I've seen no evidence that he's—"

But this time, I cut myself off, for as the two detectives led the tall man past me, I happened to look down and see the tall man had incredibly tiny feet. I also remembered what Bones had said earlier, when we'd been at the location of the first murder: something about a cab—and, therefore, a cabdriver—having been there and how two men had gone in, but not left, as friends.

Tall man. Tiny feet.

Oh. *Oh.*

CHAPTER THIRTY-SEVEN

The public detectives and the tall man were now gone, the former having wrestled the latter down the stairs and out the door. Waggins and the puppies were gone too. As for the turtle, no sooner had the door slammed behind everyone than he collapsed from sheer exhaustion right in the middle of the carpet and was now snoring.

"Well, *that* was abrupt," I said. "But wasn't that a quick wrap-up of the case?"

"Yes," Bones said, "but that is often the way of it."

"Perhaps," I said, not that I really knew—I'd

never worked on a *case* before. "But how did you know that this Mr. Jefferson Hope did it? And *why* did he do it?"

"Elementary, my dear Catson," he said. "I looked for the common thread in the case. We knew that at the first crime scene, two men went in, but only one came out. We knew there was a tall man with tiny feet—our murderer—but we also knew there was a cab. It was natural to assume someone else, a cabdriver, had driven them there. But—"

"*But,*" I said, feeling myself grow excited in a way I could never remember feeling before, not even when my life had been at risk during the Cat Wars, "when the old woman who wasn't an old woman came to claim the gold ring, and when Mr. Javier followed her in the cab later but only saw a tall man matching the description of our killer emerge, you deduced that the common thread was the cabdriver; that there wasn't, in fact, a separate cabdriver, but that the cabdriver must be our killer!"

"*Precisely,*" Bones said. "I am impressed by your perception."

"Well, you practically told me."

"Not at all, though. With the public detectives, I'd no doubt need to connect all of the dots, and still they might not get it. But you, my very dear Catson, are capable of connecting at least some of the dots all on your own."

If I could have, I'd have blushed with pride.

"So then," Bones said, "having figured that our murderer was either a cabdriver or at the very least impersonating one, I enlisted the aid of my young associates in locating him. Puppies who live on the streets have so much useful knowledge and ways of finding out whatever they don't know, because people mostly dismiss them as stupid and their presence as a nuisance."

"But what about the pills?"

"Pills?"

"Yes, the pills. When you left earlier, you said you wanted to prove that the pills were what killed er, John Smith."

"Oh." He waved a dismissive paw. "That was just a ruse. I never want the human detectives to know precisely what I'm up to until I want them to know what I'm up to. Of course I knew at least one or more of the pills contained cyanide. I could smell it."

Huh.

"So," I said, "we know who killed er, John Smith and the secretary, and how, but *why* did he do it, Bones?"

"Does it really matter?" the dog said, looking suddenly deflated.

"Does it really..." I was practically spluttering. "How can you say it doesn't matter?"

"The criminal is in custody." The dog yawned. "I've invented handcuffs." The dog yawned again. "The turtle now has a jetpack." He yawned a third time. "In the face of those three happy events, what else could possibly matter?"

"But *why* did he do it?" I insisted to know.

"*That*, my dear Catson, is a rather thorny question. And one I don't have the complete answer to as yet. Really, based on what evidence is currently available, the only motive we have is revenge, and *that* we only have because the murderer gave it to us by writing it on the walls at both crime scenes in red paint! Well, that and the fact that a woman's wedding ring was found at one of the scenes, a ring the murderer desperately wanted back. We can therefore infer that the crimes had to do with revenge over something involving a woman, but no further than that."

I stared at him for a long time. Seriously? That was all he had for me?

"Look," he finally said, "the only way we'll ever know why Jefferson Hope wanted revenge is if he tells us. And right now, he's not talking. Sometimes, my dear Catson, you need to be content with *knowing* you've caught the right person, *knowing* that you've proven how he did it, and *knowing* you've taken a very bad person off the streets and put him behind bars, unable to hurt anyone else ever again."

"And that's enough for you?" I said.

"Not really," he admitted. "But today it has to be. Tomorrow, I will rise to fight again."

I considered everything he'd said. The way he put it, it did sound like enough had been accomplished for the time being.

Then I considered how usually around midnight I need to race around my apartments, as best I can now with my bad leg, until I wear myself out in order to get to sleep at night. But it was long past midnight—hours past, in fact—and I was already worn out.

The sky outside was lightening, moving away from darkness, and soon the sun would be rising. I thought to leap onto my cozy cushion, but it was still covered in shattered glass. Mr. Javier would have to attend to that when he woke up.

As for me, I would simply curl up here on this lovely patch of carpet, like so, close my eyes and—

"What are you doing?" Bones asked.

"What does it look like I'm doing?" I asked, eyes still shut. "And shouldn't you be on your merry way by now?"

But the dog didn't reply to my question. Instead, he said eagerly, "Great! While you do that, I'll send for the rest of my things!"

"Things?" I opened one eye. "What *things?*"

"My violin, for starters."

The *dog* played the *violin*?

"Also, I was thinking," he said, sounding truly excited, "perhaps I'll take the bedroom on the left? You don't seem to use either bedroom for sleeping, but it would appear that more of your own things are in the one on the right and I wouldn't want to appear inconsiderate."

Now both my eyes were wide open.

"You're not—" I started to object, but the dog merely continued, as though I'd not spoken at all.

"And I was thinking ... " He stood there, paw to lip. "A chandelier. I think this place could use a chandelier. What do you think? Perhaps over the dining room table?"

"Bones! One last time, *you don't live here!*"

I am Dr. Jane Catson and these are my case files. That is how you know that everything you have just read is all true and not made-up stories. This is not fiction. Everything I have told you, and everything in my many case files to come, it all really happened.

ACKNOWLEDGEMENTS

I wish to thank the following people for their help along the way:

Georgia McBride, for wanting to publish a book in which it's widely accepted that animals can speak and for making the publication process so easy.

Laura Whitaker, who is such a brilliant editor, there are insufficient words for how brilliant she is. (Laura, help me out with some synonyms here!) Laura is the editor every writer dreams of: someone who sees the problem, identifies the solution and communicates it all in such a positive way, why would any sane author ever say no to her?

Everyone at the Georgia McBride Media Group – you people are rock stars.

My Friday night writing group: Lauren Catherine, Bob Gulian, Andrea Schicke Hirsch, Greg Logsted, Rob Mayette, Krissi Petersen Schooner – you make me better.

Greg Logsted and Jackie Logsted, best husband and best daughter.

Readers everywhere.

(Photo Credit: Jackie Logsted)

LAUREN BARATZ-LOGSTED

Lauren Baratz-Logsted is the author of over 25 books for adults, teens and kids, including The Sisters 8 series for young readers which she created with her husband and daughter. She lives in Danbury, CT, with that husband and daughter as well as their marvelous cat, Yoyo.

OTHER TITLES YOU MIGHT LIKE

THE ADVENTURES OF SHERLOCK BONES
CASE FILE #2:
DOG NOT GONE!

Find more books like this at Month9Books.com

Connect with us online:
Facebook: www.Facebook.com/Month9Books
Twitter: https://twitter.com/TantrumBooks
You Tube: www.youtube.com/user/Month9Books
Blog: http://month9books.tumblr.com/

CASE FILE #2
THE ADVENTURES OF
SHERLOCK BONES
DOG NOT GONE!
LAUREN BARATZ-LOGSTED
AUTHOR OF THE SISTERS 8 SERIES